Contents

A Little Princess

Frances Hodgson Burnett was born with the name
Frances Eliza Hodgson in England in the nineteenth
century. Her father, like Sara's father in this story, died
when Frances was young, leaving very little money.
Unlike Sara, however, Frances had a mother, two
brothers and two sisters, and together they moved
to America to start a new life on a farm. Frances
later married Dr Burnett and took the name Frances
Hodgson Burnett. She became famous for writing
about the working conditions of very poor people,
such as Becky in this book.

Frances Hodgson Burnett's

A little Princess

Adapted by KATE PETTY

Illustrated by Alan Marks

This adaptation © 2001 Kate Petty
Illustrations copyright © 2001 Alan Marks

A Little Princess first published in Great Britain in 1905

This adaptation published in 2001 for WHSmith,
Greenbridge Road, Swindon, SN3 3LD
by Hodder Children's Books

A Catalogue record for this book is available from the British Library

ISBN 0 340 85273 9

Typeset by Avon Dataset Ltd, Bidford-on-Avon, Warks

Printed and bound in Great Britain by
The Guernsey Press Co. Ltd, Channel Isles

Hodder Children's Books
a division of Hodder Headline Limited
338 Euston Road
London NW1 3BH

1

Sara

Let us go back more than a hundred years to a murky winter afternoon in London. A gas-lit time when the dark cobbled streets were more shadow than light, when the city sounds were of horses' hooves and rumbling carts and stallholders' cries. When Queen Victoria was on the throne and her empire stretched to the farthest corners of the world.

A horse-drawn carriage is trundling

through these foggy, bumpy streets, and in it are two people who are nearly at the end of a long, long journey. A dark-haired little girl and her handsome father have travelled for weeks across the sea from their home in India. The girl is Sara Crewe, who is only seven years old, though she is tall for her age and looks older. She cuddles up to her father and gazes at the streets outside. Soon he will have to leave her behind at her new school and travel back to India alone.

At last the carriage draws up outside a tall brick building. It looks just like all the other buildings in the square except for a brass plate saying MISS MINCHIN, SELECT SEMINARY FOR YOUNG LADIES. 'Is this the place?' Sara asks her father.

'Yes, my darling. We are here,' he says as he lifts her down from the carriage. The two of them climb the steps to the front door and ring the bell.

* * *

Sara and her father both tried to be cheerful as they waited to meet the new headmistress. Sara looked around her at the cold, hard room that was so very different from the warm, bright places she'd left behind. Sara's French mother had died when she was a baby, but Sara had been brought up surrounded by kind servants who gave her everything she wanted. You might think she'd have been spoilt, but Sara was an affectionate, thoughtful little girl, who liked nothing more than to bury her nose in a book or to make up beautiful stories for herself.

'I don't like it much,' she whispered to her father, 'but I suppose I'll just have to put up with it – like a soldier puts up with going into battle.'

Captain Crewe laughed and hugged the little girl he was going to miss so much. Just then Miss Minchin came into the room.

Miss Minchin had large, cold, fishy eyes and a large, cold, fishy smile which she directed at Sara. She knew that Captain Crewe was a very rich man with plenty of money to lavish on his beloved daughter. 'It will be a great honour to have such a promising and beautiful student,' she said, taking Sara's hand and stroking it.

She doesn't really think I'm beautiful, thought Sara. She's only saying it for Papa.

Sara was to have her own rooms at the school, a French maid and a pony and carriage to herself.

'I'm not the least bit worried about her education,' said Captain Crewe proudly. 'Sara gobbles up books like a wolf, Miss Minchin. In fact, it's more important that you make her ride her pony or go out and buy a new doll.'

'But Papa,' Sara interrupted, 'I don't want a lot of dolls. Just one special one, to be a good friend – like Emily is going to be.'

Miss Minchin looked puzzled. 'And who is Emily?' she asked.

'Emily is the doll I am going to buy,' said Sara. 'She will be my friend when my papa has gone.'

Miss Minchin smiled her fishy smile. 'What a darling, original child,' she said.

'Yes, she is,' said Sara's papa. 'You must take great care of her for me, Miss Minchin.'

The next few days were spent shopping. Sara and her papa bought so many velvet dresses trimmed with fur and lace, and hats with ostrich feathers, and silk stockings and handkerchiefs and boxes of gloves that the shop assistants began to think Sara must be quite a little princess.

On the last day, as they were going into yet another toy shop, Sara pointed excitedly and said, 'That's Emily!' And there sat a beautiful doll, not too big to carry about, with long, golden-brown hair and grey-blue eyes with real eyelashes and a nice, interested sort of expression. So Emily was bought, and she too was fitted out with a wardrobe of silk dresses and boots and furs.

And then it was time to say goodbye. Captain Crewe saw Sara searching his face with her strange, grey-green eyes. 'Are you learning me by heart, little Sara?' he asked.

'I know you by heart,' she replied. 'You are inside my heart.' And then they hugged and kissed as if they never wanted to let each other go.

By the time Sara went into lessons the next morning, everyone was talking about the new girl who was going to be Miss Minchin's star pupil. 'But I heard Miss Minchin say that her clothes are far too grand for a child,' said Lavinia Herbert spitefully to her friend Jessie.

'She isn't pretty like some girls,' said Jessie, finding it harder to be critical, 'but she does have lovely long eyelashes.'

Miss Minchin came into the classroom. 'Young ladies,' she said, 'I should like to introduce you to your new companion.' All the girls stood up. 'I expect you all to make Miss Crewe very welcome, as she has come from a long way away, India in fact. You can get to know one another when lessons are over.'

Sara gave a little curtsey and the other girls bowed, and then everyone sat down and stared at her some more.

The first lesson was French. Miss Minchin called Sara up to the front and handed her a text book. 'Since your father has given you a French maid,' she said, 'I expect that he is very keen for you to learn French.'

'I think,' said Sara, embarrassed, 'that he simply thought I'd like her.'

Miss Minchin looked at her sharply.

'What a spoilt little thing you are,' she said, 'to imagine that everything is just for your pleasure. No, I am sure he wanted you to learn French.'

'I've never really learned French,' began Sara, who had spoken French all her life, 'but—'

'No buts,' said Miss Minchin as Sara flushed and stopped trying to explain.

'Now don't sulk, Sara. I'm sure you'll like learning French.'

Miss Minchin spoke to the French teacher as soon as he arrived. 'This is your new pupil, monsieur,' she said, 'but she seems to have taken against the French language already.'

'I'm sorry to hear that,' said the French teacher, who was a kind man.

Sara was feeling quite desperate by now. She stood up and started to explain to him – in French – that she had never learned French out of books, but that her dear mamma, who had died, was French, and that she couldn't remember a time when she didn't know how to speak it.

The French teacher was charmed by this little girl who spoke his language so perfectly. He turned to Miss Minchin and said, 'There isn't much I can teach this child, madame. She hasn't learned French because she *is* French.'

Miss Minchin looked icy. 'Why didn't you tell me, child?' she said crossly to Sara.

'I did try,' said Sara. 'But I suppose I – I didn't start off right,' she faltered, as the other girls started to titter.

'Silence, girls!' shouted Miss Minchin, rapping the desk. 'Silence, I say!' She was already starting to take a dislike to her show pupil.

2

Ermengarde and Lottie

Something else happened during that
first French lesson. Ermengarde, a plump
little girl who was not very bright, was
so astonished to hear someone her own
age speaking fluent French that she started
chewing the ribbon on her blonde plait.
Miss Minchin scolded her in front of the
whole class, which made the other girls
snigger.

Now Sara hated injustice. And when she

saw poor Ermengarde blush, and tears start into her blue eyes, it made her want to protect her. So after the lesson was over Sara went and sat with her on the window seat. 'What's your name?' she asked in a friendly way.

Ermengarde's blue eyes widened. 'Ermengarde St John,' she replied timidly.

'That's a pretty name,' said Sara. Ermengarde couldn't think of anything else to say. It wasn't every day that such a clever girl who wore expensive clothes and came all the way from India took any notice of you.

Sara tried again. 'Would you like to see Emily?'

'Who's Emily?' whispered Ermengarde.

'You can come up and meet her if you like,' said Sara.

So Ermengarde puffed up the stairs after Sara. 'Do you really have your own playroom?' she asked her.

'Yes,' said Sara. 'My father wanted me to have one because he knows that I like to tell myself stories and don't want anyone listening.'

'Can you really make up stories?'

'It's not hard,' said Sara, and then, as they stood outside the door she turned back to Ermengarde with her finger over her lips. 'Shhh! We might manage to surprise her this time.'

Sara flung open the door. 'Oh, bother,' she said. 'I thought we might catch her, you see, before she made it back into her chair.'

Ermengarde saw a beautiful doll in a chair with a book placed in her arms. 'Is that Emily?' she asked. 'Can she really walk?'

'Of course,' said Sara. 'Well, of course I pretend she can. So that makes me think it's true.'

The next hour was the most exciting Ermengarde had ever spent as she sat by

Sara's fire, holding Emily and listening to Sara telling her about the wonderful magical things she liked to believe. But there was one moment when Sara was talking about Papa buying Emily that she drew her breath in sharply, as if she had a pain.

'Are you all right, Sara?' asked Ermengarde, alarmed.

'It's just – Do you love your father very much?' Sara said.

Ermengarde, whose clever father was in fact not very nice to his disappointing daughter, said, 'I don't see mine very often.'

'Well, I love my father more than the world ten times over – and he has gone away.' Sara went on quickly, 'But talking to you about pretending helps. It doesn't make me forget him, but it helps.'

Ermengarde had decided to ask Sara something, even though it looked as though she might be about to cry. 'Lavinia and Jessie are best friends,' she said huskily. 'Could I be yours? Even though you're the cleverest girl in the school and I'm the stupidest?'

'Of course!' said Sara, smiling again. 'And I'll help you with your lessons if you like.'

A few weeks later, Sara made another friend.

She had settled down into school routine. With all her luxuries she sometimes seemed more like an honoured guest than another pupil, but it didn't seem to affect her. Even Jessie was heard to say to Lavinia, 'You know, Lavvy, Sara never acts grand – though I think I would if people made that much fuss of me.'

'Well, I think it's absolutely disgusting the way Miss Minchin shows her off,' Lavinia retorted. " 'Dear Sara, come and tell Lady So-and-so about India . . . Oh, do let's hear dear Sara speaking French'." Lavinia was jealous, of course, though it was true to say that such a clever pupil was very useful to Miss Minchin.

Sara was coming down the stairs one day when she heard Lottie from the nursery class throwing a tantrum. Miss Minchin and her sister Amelia were trying to deal with her, but Miss Minchin soon gave up and strode grimly from the room. She saw Sara and put on a smile.

'I think I might be able to handle Lottie, Miss Minchin, said Sara. 'Would you let me try?'

Miss Minchin agreed, grudgingly, and Sara went in. The little girl was beating her fists on the floor and wailing pitifully – as she always did, because it usually got her what she wanted – 'I haven't got a mummy any more . . . I haven't got a mummy any more . . .'

'Neither have I,' said Sara, when Lottie paused to draw breath.

Surprised, Lottie opened her eyes and stopped yelling. 'Where's your mamma then?' she asked.

Now Sara had thought a lot about where her poor dead mother was, and had a very good picture in her head of heaven. She started to describe it to Lottie. 'She's in heaven, where there are fields and fields of flowers, and a soft wind that blows the lovely scent around. No one is ever tired there, because they can float wherever they like. They can float to the walls that are made of pearl and gold and send beautiful messages down to people on earth.'

'I want to go there,' said Lottie, still sniffing a little. 'I haven't got a mummy—'

'I tell you what,' said Sara before Lottie started again, 'I'll be your mummy at school. And my doll Emily can be your sister. Would you like that? Let's go and tell her now – then we can brush your hair.'

So Lottie trotted after Sara, quite forgetting that having her hair brushed was what started the tantrum in the first place.

3

Becky

Sara was popular at school. Lavinia and Jessie never liked her but the other girls loved her. It wasn't because she was the show pupil, or because she had such lovely clothes, but because she told such wonderful stories. When Sara told a story the pupils at Miss Minchin's could forget for a while that they were at boarding school or that they were homesick. For a short time they could lose themselves in a fairyland of princesses or in an underwater world with mermaids and sea-kings.

When Sara had been at the school for about two years, a new girl came into her life. Becky wasn't a pupil, but a scullery maid, the lowest sort of servant, who ran up and downstairs all day carrying heavy buckets of coal and was shouted at by everyone from the teachers to the cook. Sara noticed that Becky tried to stay in the room when she was telling stories one day, putting coal on the fire piece by piece, so that she could linger a little longer. Lavinia and Jessie noticed too. 'That girl has been listening,' said Lavinia. 'I don't think your mamma would like you to tell stories to servant girls, Sara,' she added cruelly, knowing perfectly well that Sara had no mother. 'I know *mine* wouldn't.'

'I don't think my mother would mind at all,' retorted Sara. 'She knows that stories belong to everybody.'

* * *

On a cold, foggy afternoon, rather like the one on which she had first arrived, Sara went into her own little sitting room to change out of the pretty, rose-coloured dress she'd been wearing for dancing class. There, fast asleep in the armchair in front of the warm fire, was Becky. Her maid's cap was askew and her mouth hung open. Sara looked at the poor, exhausted little thing and didn't know what to do. If Miss Amelia chose to come in, Becky would be in terrible trouble. But then a burning coal shifted in the fireplace and Becky woke up in fright.

'Oh, miss!' she said to Sara, 'I beg your pardon, I really do! I didn't mean to! I only sat down for a minute, miss!'

Sara said kindly, 'You were tired. It wasn't your fault.'

It was obvious that Becky had never known gentleness or kindness in her life and Sara suddenly felt unbearably sorry for

her. She touched Becky's cheek. 'We're just the same really,' she said thoughtfully. 'I'm only a little girl like you. It's just an accident that I'm not you and you're not me.'

Poor Becky didn't know what Sara was talking about. She stared at her in her silk dancing dress. 'You look like a princess, miss,' she said. 'I saw a princess, once, going into the opera house in Covent Garden, and she looked like you, miss.'

Then Sara had an idea. 'You never heard the end of that story in the school room, did you Becky? I can't finish it for you now, but if you tell me what time you get to my room, I'll try and be here, and I can tell you a little bit more each day. Would you like that?'

As Becky went off, happier that she had ever been, Sara thought about being a princess. If I pretend to be a princess, she told herself, I can invent little things to do that will make people happier.

In fact, recent news from India made it seem that Sara might indeed be about to become as rich as a princess before long. Her father wrote that he'd had a visit from a very dear old schoolfriend. The schoolfriend had discovered diamonds on his land, and wanted Captain Crewe to go into the diamond-mining business with him. Business matters didn't interest Sara at all, but underground tunnels filled with sparkling diamonds did sound romantic. Soon she had everyone listening to stories about them.

Lavinia and Jessie didn't know what to think about the diamond mines. 'Perhaps Sara will be so rich that she will be ridiculous,' Jessie giggled nervously to Lavinia.

'She's already ridiculous without being rich,' sniffed Lavinia in return.

To Becky, Sara was always a princess. Soon they chatted and laughed as real friends, though there was all the difference in the world between their lives. When Becky told Sara she was 'nice', Sara said she was only nice because life had always been kind to her. 'I don't know how I shall ever find out whether I'm really nice or completely horrible, because I've never had to face any real trials, like you have, Becky.'

Trials like the rats in her attic bedroom, and never enough food to eat, and always being cold in bed.

4

The diamond mines

Sara's eleventh birthday was approaching, and Miss Minchin – with the diamond mines in mind – had been told to spare no expense. In fact, Sara had been a little worried by her father's most recent letter. He wrote that he wasn't very well – he found it hard to sleep with all those horrible facts and figures going round in his head.

'If my Little Missus were here,' he said, 'I dare say she'd give me some good advice!'

Little Missus was one of his pet names for Sara.

Sara's present was to be another special doll, because, as she wrote back to her father, 'Soon I will be eleven years old, and no one will give me another doll because I'll be too old, so this one will be the Last Doll.'

On the morning of her birthday Sara found a funny little parcel in her room. It was wrapped in brown paper and tied with string. Inside was a lumpy pin-cushion, lovingly made from some not quite clean red material. The pins had been stuck in to spell MENNY HAPY RETURNS. Sara knew that Becky would have sat up late at night to make this for her.

'It ain't nothin', miss,' said Becky, 'but I knew you could pretend it was satin with diamond pins in.'

Sara threw her arms round Becky, 'Oh, Becky, I do love you,' she cried.

The schoolroom was decorated with holly

for the party and Miss Minchin was wearing her grandest silk dress. Three servants, one of them Becky, made a procession into the room with Sara's presents as the girls crowded round excitedly.

Then Miss Minchin left and the Last Doll and her fabulous clothes were unwrapped and passed round. Even Lavinia and Jessie were so enchanted that they forgot that they were supposed to be too old for dolls.

Just then, Miss Amelia came into the room looking anxious. 'Girls,' she said, 'you are to have your tea now in the parlour. Sara's father's solicitor has arrived, and Miss Minchin needs to speak to him alone in here.' The girls rushed into the parlour for tea and Miss Minchin escorted the solicitor into the schoolroom.

'The *late* Captain Crewe?' Miss Minchin was saying. 'You mean that Captain Crewe is dead?'

'Died of jungle fever and business

troubles combined. Ruined. His best friend took all his money for the diamond mines and then ran away.

'Do you mean that that child, whose ridiculous birthday party I have just paid for myself, is a beggar? And that she is left on my hands?'

'There certainly isn't anyone else to look after her,' said the solicitor. 'We're not responsible for her. Captain Crewe died without paying our bill.'

'But this is monstrous!' said Miss Minchin. 'I've been cheated! I'll turn her out into the street.'

'I don't think that would look very good for the school,' said the solicitor. 'Better to keep her and make use of her.'

When he had gone, Miss Minchin called her sister. 'Tell Sara Crewe to put on a black dress,' she said, 'and come and see me.'

'I'm not sure she has a black dress,' said Amelia, puzzled.

'Her father is dead,' said Miss Minchin, 'and that spoilt child won't be wearing fine clothes again. Explain to her clearly that I will have no crying or unpleasant scenes.'

A few hours later Sara stood before Miss Minchin. The party seemed like a long-ago dream. She was dressed in a black dress that was far too small for her and she was clutching Emily. 'What do you mean by bringing that doll with you?' said Miss Minchin. 'Put her down.'

'No, I won't,' said Sara quietly. 'My papa gave her to me and she is all I have left.'

'You'll have no time for dolls now,' said Miss Minchin. 'From now on you are a beggar. Your maid has been dismissed and your pony and carriage have been sent away. You will wear only your oldest and plainest clothes, and you are to sleep in the attic room next to Becky's.'

So Sara climbed the stairs to another world. She sat down on the hard bed under the skylight in the bare room. She didn't cry, but held Emily on her lap and laid her dark head on her, and stayed there not making a sound. It wasn't until Becky crept in to comfort her that she allowed herself to sob. 'Oh, Becky,' she said, 'I told you we were just the same – just two little girls. And now it's true. I'm not a princess any more.'

'Oh, but you are, miss,' cried Becky. 'Whatever happens to you, Miss Sara, you'll always be a princess.'

5

In the attic

My papa is dead. My papa is dead, was the only thought in Sara's head on that first terrible night in the attic. So numb with grief was she that she didn't even notice the hardness of the bed, the wildness of the dark night or the scrabblings of the mice and rats.

Everything had changed. Miss Minchin wanted Sara to be in no doubt from the very start that she was now a servant.

When she went down to breakfast the next morning, wearing the black dress that was too small, she was sent to keep the little ones in order. 'You're already too late,' said Miss Minchin crossly. 'Lottie has spilt her tea.'

Sara was expected to help the younger girls with their French and hear their other lessons. And to run errands like an errand-boy and clean rooms like a housemaid. Because she was clever, she could deliver complicated messages, or pay bills and come back with the correct change.

At first Sara tried to be a willing helper. But her willingness only made the other servants find more and more jobs for her. Soon she was running about all day at everyone's beck and call. She started to look very tired and pale.

After working all day she went to the schoolroom late at night to study and then crept up to her cold attic to sleep.

With both parents dead, a wretchedly hard life and no friends to talk to, she felt completely alone.

It's not quite true to say that Sara had no friends at all. After a while Becky managed to slip into her room sometimes. 'Don't mind if I don't talk to you when we're working,' she said. 'It's not worth us both being told off.'

So what about Ermengarde, Sara's 'best friend'?

One day, when Sara was loaded down with laundry, she and Ermengarde ran into each other in a corridor. Ermengarde had been away for a while, and she was so shocked to see her friend looking like a servant that she didn't know what to say. 'Oh, Sara, is that you?' she said, stupidly.

'Yes,' said Sara, and narrowed her eyes at Ermengarde over the pile of clothes. She's just like all the others, she thought. She doesn't want to know me.

'Are – are you –' Ermengarde stuttered, trying so hard to think of the right thing to say, 'very unhappy?'

'What do you think?' snapped Sara. 'Do you think I'm happy?' And she marched past her old friend without another word.

Ermengarde was desperate. She hadn't meant to upset Sara. She sat on her window seat and cried.

Late one night, Sara climbed the stairs to her attic long after the pupils had gone to bed. There was light coming from under the door. I wonder who could be in there? she thought. She opened the door cautiously and was frightened to see a figure huddled on her bed in a red shawl. It was Ermengarde.

'Ermengarde!' she said. And then – 'You'll get into terrible trouble if you're caught.'

'I don't care if I get into trouble,' said Ermengarde. 'I just want to know what's wrong, Sara. Why don't you like me any more?'

'Well,' Sara hesitated. 'It's just that you're different.'

'Me, different?' exclaimed Ermengarde. 'It's you that's different, Sara! You won't talk to me!'

Sara was silent for a few minutes. 'You're right, Ermengarde,' she said. 'I am different now. None of the other girls want to talk to me. I thought you were the same. But I was wrong.'

'Oh, Sara,' wailed Ermengarde. 'You might not need me, but without you I was so lost. And then tonight I thought – why don't I just go up and see her? I so much want us to be friends again.'

The two girls hugged each other tightly.

'You're nicer than I am,' said Sara. 'I once said that if I had to suffer I might not be a nice person any more. And I'm not. I doubted you. Perhaps that was the point of me having to suffer.'

'I don't think anyone should have to suffer like you do,' said Ermengarde. 'Oh, Sara, do you think you can bear to live up here?'

Sara looked around. 'I can pretend it's the Bastille,' she said, 'and that I'm a prisoner of the French Revolution. Becky is the prisoner in the next cell.'

Ermengarde's eyes widened. She adored Sara's stories. 'Will you tell me all about it?'

'Well,' said Sara, 'Miss Minchin is the jailer . . . ' and her eyes shone for the first time. Her imagination was beginning to work for her at last.

6

Melchisedec

Sara did have another friend amongst Miss Minchin's pupils – one who missed her a lot, and who was too young to understand the change in her 'mamma'. Lottie tried to talk to Sara in lesson time, but Sara had to hush her for fear of Miss Minchin scolding her.

Lottie was a determined child. Late one afternoon she climbed up more stairs than she had ever climbed before and arrived at two doors. Bravely she pushed one open and saw her beloved Sara standing on a table with her head out of the skylight.

Lottie was horrified at the bare little room. 'Sara!' she cried, running to the table.

Lottie's sudden appearance gave Sara a fright. What if she howled or yelled and Miss Minchin heard her? She jumped down from the table. 'Oh, please don't make a noise, Lottie. Or we'll be caught – and I've already been shouted at so many times today.' Lottie looked at her fearfully and Sara tried to calm her. 'It's not such a bad room, really,' she said comfortingly. 'I've got my own little world up here, you know,' she added bravely, seeing Lottie's lip tremble.

'Can I see it?' Lottie asked, longing to be drawn into Sara's world.

'Let's get up on the table, then,' said Sara, and soon both she and Lottie were standing with their heads out of the skylight window. It was indeed another world up there amongst the chimneys and the roof slates, with the streets and busy people so far below. 'Look Lottie, there's a sparrow. If I had some crumbs I'd get him to come closer.'

'I've got some crumbs,' said Lottie, excitedly pulling a bit of bun from her pocket.

Sara tossed a few crumbs on to the slates.

'Be very quiet, Lottie. We want the sparrow to trust us.'

The sparrow put his head on one side and looked at them. Then he darted forward to pick up the crumbs. 'See?' whispered Sara. 'Now his friend will come too.' Before long there were two sparrows chattering and quarrelling right by them.

'I'd love to live up here,' said Lottie. But Sara soon had to persuade her to go downstairs to her own room. When she had gone, Sara sat down on her battered stool and felt lonelier than ever.

Just then a little movement caught Sara's attention. She kept very still and saw a rat sitting on his hind legs sniffing the air. Like the sparrows, the rat sensed that this little girl wasn't going to hurt him. He was hungry and desperate for the crumbs that Lottie had dropped. He nibbled them quickly and then hesitated. The biggest bit was right by Sara's feet.

I do believe he wants that bit for his children, thought Sara, and hardly dared to breathe as the rat darted in and snatched it up before scurrying back to his family under the floorboards.

He's a nice rat, thought Sara. I'd like to make a friend of him. That's what prisoners in the Bastille did sometimes.

So over the next week she managed to take up some stale crusts with her and coaxed him out until he was no longer afraid.

It wasn't easy for Ermengarde and Lottie to come and visit Sara without being seen. But one evening, when Ermengarde had made her way upstairs and tapped lightly on Sara's door, there was no answer. She listened at the keyhole and heard Sara speaking in a low voice. 'Who were you talking to?' she asked, when Sara let her in.

'I'll tell you if you promise not to scream,' said Sara.

'I won't,' said Ermengarde. 'Who was it?'

'My rat, Melchisedec.'

Ermengarde managed not to scream, but she leapt on to the bed quick as a flash. 'A rat?' she said.

'He's a very polite rat,' said Sara, 'and he has a family to feed. Do you want to meet him?'

'All right,' said Ermengarde nervously and sat tight as Sara called to Melchisedec and put out some crumbs for him. But then she watched amazed as the creature came out and looked at them with his intelligent beady eyes before taking the crumbs away with him.

'Listen,' said Sara. 'You can hear his wife and children squeaking to say thank you.'

'You make him seem real, Sara,' said Ermengarde. 'You talk about him as if he was a person.'

'He is, really,' said Sara. 'He has a family and he gets hungry, just like us. That's why

I gave him a name. I think he's a Bastille rat, sent to be my friend.'

'Oh, Sara,' said Ermengarde, thrilled. 'You make it all seem like a wonderful story!'

'It is a story,' said Sara. 'We're all part of a story, you, me, Miss Minchin . . .' and she talked on until she had to make Ermengarde leave the world of the Bastille to go unwillingly downstairs to her own comfortable room.

7

The Montmerencys

Apart from the occasional visits from Ermengarde and Lottie, Sara spent most of her days alone. Up in her attic room she had the sparrows and Melchisedec's family for company, but running errands through the cold, wet streets she had no one.

Some days people only spoke to her to tell her off. In her outgrown, shabby clothes she passed unnoticed by the rest of the world. Once or twice she caught sight of herself in a shop window and almost laughed at the scarecrow figure she had become. But during that winter her life was no laughing matter. She had holes in her shoes and she was often chilled to the bone.

One of the things that kept Sara going was looking into people's houses – at that time in the evening when the lamps are on but the curtains are not yet drawn. She imagined the sort of lives that went on behind those windows. She was particularly interested by a large family who lived in her square. There were eight children, and from the red flowery wallpaper and comfortable furniture Sara thought theirs must be a cheerful home. She called them the Montmerencys and always looked out for them. Soon she knew the eight children apart, and gave each one of them a fanciful first name too.

One evening close to Christmas, a funny thing happened. As Sara was returning from the shops, the Montmerency children were crossing the pavement to their carriage. They were dressed in their best clothes for a Christmas party. They looked so enchanting in their lace dresses and bows that Sara stopped to watch. Sweetest of all was the little boy with gold curls and a sailor suit. Now, because it was Christmas-time, the children had heard many stories about giving to the poor, and the little boy saw his chance to be generous. Here was a little beggar girl watching him hungrily.

He wasn't to know that Sara was hungry for the warmth of family life rather than food.

'Here, poor little girl,' said the five-year-old kindly, 'have this coin and buy yourself some food.'

Sara was horrified. She'd been mistaken for a beggar! 'Thank you, no!' she said. 'I couldn't take your money!' But then she

realised that the little boy would be hurt if his kind offer was turned down.

His sisters turned back to listen.

'Oh, all right,' Sara relented. 'You're a really kind little boy. Thank you.' She took the coin from him and put it in her pocket. But her eyes filled with tears at the thought of what she had become.

Later, the Montmerency children (whose

surname was really Carmichael) were talking about her in their carriage. 'She didn't speak like a beggar,' said Janet, the oldest.

'And she didn't really have a beggar's face,' said Nora, the next one down.

'Well, I gave her all my money,' said Donald, the little boy, proudly, 'and she said I was a really kind little boy.'

'She works at the school,' said Janet. 'I think she's probably an orphan, but she isn't a beggar.'

From then on the family were as interested in Sara as she was in them. They called her 'the-little-girl-who-is-not-a beggar'.

But still Sara was lonely. Emily, her doll, sometimes seemed to mock her with her silence. After one long, hard day, when Sara came in wet and cold, Emily was no comfort at all. Sara knocked her from her chair. 'You're nothing but a doll!' she cried. 'You've never had a heart. You'll never be able to feel!' And poor Sara sobbed and sobbed as her doll lay feet-over-head on the floor.

Imagine Sara's delight when she saw a removal van outside the house next door.

If only I could see their furniture, she thought, I'd know what sort of neighbours we're going to have. Miss Minchin's furniture is cold and hard like she is, and the Montmerency's furniture is warm and cheerful just like them.

Sara was sent out again late in the day and came back to see some furniture waiting on the pavement. Her heart gave a little jump. There was an Indian carved desk and some rolled-up Indian rugs! Perhaps the new neighbours had some connection with the country where she'd been born.

Later still, Sara was fetching in the evening milk when she saw Mr Montmerency running up the steps to the new neighbour's front door.

Perhaps the Montmerencys are their friends, she thought, and there will be lots of children and they'll all play in the attic together, and I'll meet them.

Becky had more information at bedtime. 'It's a Nindian gentlemen,' she told Sara. 'At least, he lived in Nindia but he looks like an Englishman to me. He's rich and he's ill, because he's had a lot of trouble. The father of the large family is his lawyer.'

It was some weeks before Sara saw the Indian gentleman. A carriage pulled up, and from it emerged first Mr Montmerency, then a nurse and two Indian men-servants. The man they carried from the carriage was as thin as a skeleton. It was clear to Sara that the Indian gentleman was very ill indeed.

8

Ram Dass

The good things about Sara's attic bedroom brought a little joy into her sad life. Standing with her head out of the skylight made her feel closer to the sky and the birds and fresh air. But the real treat came if there was a beautiful sunset. Downstairs, or out in the street, you could only catch a glimpse of a sunset, but from the attic window Sara could revel in its full glory.

One evening, soon after the Indian

gentleman had moved in next door, Sara saw the golden light of a sunset reflected in the windows and managed to escape upstairs. She climbed on to her table and stood with her head out of the window. It's so beautiful, she thought. It made her feel as if magic might be about to happen.

A strange sound made her turn. It was a squeaky, chattering sound – one that Sara had not heard for a long time. She saw, emerging from the next-door skylight, the white-turbaned head of an Indian man-servant, who was holding a chattering pet monkey in his arms. Sara smiled at the young man kindly. He nodded and saluted her – and let go of the monkey.

The monkey leapt across the roof slates and hopped past Sara through the skylight into her room. Sara laughed – she was thrilled to see a monkey. But she knew she'd have to give him back, so, without thinking, she spoke to the Indian in his own language. He was so surprised by this that his words came out all in a rush. He said that the monkey was a naughty little creature, but not bad, and perhaps it would be best if he, Ram Dass, came and fetched the monkey from Sara's room himself.

So Ram Dass climbed out of one skylight window and into the next. He landed lightly in Sara's room and soon the monkey was clinging to him again. He thanked Sara, and then was gone as quickly as he had arrived.

After he had gone, Sara sat down to think. The Indian and the monkey had stirred many memories of a childhood that had quite disappeared. Ram Dass must have noticed her bare attic room but he had treated her with great respect – like the daughter of a prince. Sara dimly remembered a time when everyone had treated her like that. Now all anyone did was shout at her.

Then Sara had a thought which made her lift her chin and straighten her back. She remembered how much it helped her when she behaved like a princess. It was much harder to act like a princess if you were dressed in rags and tatters, but so much more of a triumph!

The next day Sara was collecting up the French books from the nursery class that she taught. She was thinking about kings and queens in disguise. King Alfred had been in disguise when he burnt the cakes and had his ears boxed by the shepherd's wife. How dreadful she must have felt when she realised!

Sara imagined how Miss Minchin would feel if she found out that Sara was really a princess all along. Would she be frightened of the mistreated little girl whose shoes were full of holes? She looked over at Miss Minchin with narrowed eyes.

w Miss Minchin hated that look! It made her so cross that she boxed Sara's ears.

Sara was shocked. She stood still for a moment and then let out a nervous little laugh.

'What are you laughing at?' cried Miss Minchin, angrier than ever.

'I was thinking,' Sara replied.

'Apologise at once!' said Miss Minchin.

Sara looked at her. 'I will apologise for laughing,' she said, 'but not for thinking.'

'How dare you think!' shouted Miss Minchin. 'What were you thinking?'

By now all the class were listening and nudging each other.

'I was thinking,' said Sara coolly, 'that you didn't know what you were doing.'

'I beg your pardon?' said Miss Minchin.

'I was thinking what you'd do if you'd just boxed my ears and then discovered that you'd boxed the ears of a real princess who could have you executed for it if she wanted.'

Miss Minchin was speechless. For a brief moment she'd been caught up in Sara's imagination. Then she recovered. 'Go to your room at once!' she shouted. 'Get on with your work, girls.'

'Didn't Sara look odd?' whispered Jessie to Lavinia. 'Sometimes I wouldn't be surprised if we discovered she really was someone special after all.'

9

Six penny buns

Winter was coming and darkness fell while Sara was still busy on her errands. Though there were now no sunsets to watch and the skylight window had to be shut tight against the rain, Sara still liked to look into the lighted windows in the square. Her attic room was cold and damp, but the lights in the Montemerencys' house cheered her, and the warm glow from the Indian gentleman's study was rich and inviting.

She often stood out in the cold just to watch him through the window. Sometimes she thought the monkey looked homesick, but the gentleman was clearly ill and she felt sorry for him.

'I have adopted the Indian gentleman for a friend,' she told Becky. The servants and kitchen staff often gossiped about the new neighbour, and Sara found out quite a bit more by listening to them. His name was Mr Carrisford, and he wasn't an Indian gentleman at all, but an Englishman who had spent many years in India. It seemed that, like Captain Crewe, he had also lost a lot of money in the mines, and was now recovering from an illness.

When Sara looked at his tired face under the lamp-light it seemed to her that something else was still bothering him. Probably the doctors and nurses who visited him knew what it was. Sara thought that Mr Montmorency might know too, because he was often in and out of the house.

In fact, Mr Carrisford knew quite a lot about Sara. Ram Dass had told him about the little girl in the attic bedroom next door. What's more, Janet and Nora (the Montmorency girls) had told him about the-little-girl-who-isn't-a-beggar. These stories about poor little girls upset Mr Carrisford, and this is why.

The shock of losing all his money had made Mr Carrisford ill, and he ran away. He got better, only to find that his best friend and partner in the business had died. Then he learned that he hadn't lost the money after all – the business had done well and he was rich beyond his dreams. His partner would also have been rich, and so would his partner's only child – but he didn't know where to find her. Back in England, the hopeless search for the child was making him iller than ever. He didn't even know her first name.

Mr Carmichael (that is what we must call Mr Montmerency now) was Mr Carrisford's lawyer, and he was helping him with the search. One day the news was good – they had tracked down a school in France where a little girl from India with a French mother and an English father had been sent. The parents of the little girl at the French school had died, and she had been adopted. Then it seemed that she had been taken to live in Moscow. Mr Carrisford was excited – and so were Janet and Nora, who were longing for her to be found.

Mr Carmichael tried to calm them down. 'Let me follow up this lead, at least,' he said to Mr Carrisford. 'You are sure that she went to school in France, aren't you?'

'Not completely sure, no,' said Mr Carrisford anxiously. 'I only know that her mother was French and that her father wanted her to speak French. Whenever we were together we only talked about business. But wait –' he scratched his head – 'he did have a funny little pet name for her. I don't remember him ever calling her by a name, but he did sometimes talk about "the Little Missus".'

'Don't worry,' said Mr Carmichael. 'I'm almost sure that we will find Captain Crewe's daughter safe and sound in Moscow, and I will bring her back with me. You will have her at your side in a matter of weeks.'

That day had been one of Sara's worst. She was growing fast, and her clothes were all too small. They were also too thin for the bitter weather, and her shoes let in so much water that she might as well not have worn them. She'd gone out into the wet so many times that her dress was covered in mud and she was wet through. Everyone was bad-tempered and Cook had sent her out yet again, without any lunch.

At times like these, it was harder than usual for Sara to imagine herself a princess, well fed and warmly clothed. She stood waiting to cross the road and thought up a wonderful daydream to help her get through the next few hours.

Suppose I found a sixpence, she thought, and there was a baker's shop with buns. I could walk in and buy six penny buns and eat them!

And then she spotted it! A silver coin! It was only a fourpence, and most people wouldn't have seen it underfoot.

She picked it up and crossed the road to – of all things – a baker's shop. I suppose I'd better check that no one has reported it missing, thought Sara, and went towards the door. A little bundle of rags caught her eye. It was a beggar girl – her cold red-purple feet stuck out. If I was a real princess, said Sara to herself, I would give food to starving people like that.

She went into the shop and asked about the fourpence. The woman in the shop could see that Sara was hungry. 'Keep it,' she said. 'What would you like?'

'Four penny buns, please,' said Sara, and looked surprised when the woman put six into the bag.

'I've only got four pence,' she said.

'The other two will make up the weight,' said the shop woman and watched curiously as Sara left the shop. She saw Sara stoop down to the beggar child and give her five of the six buns.

Well I never, she thought. It's not as if she wasn't hungry herself.

Sara ate the remaining bun slowly, imagining that each bite was a whole plateful of food. She made her way back to the square, but drew back when she saw

the large family gathered in their doorway. They were waving their father off on a journey. A carriage with his cases was waiting in the road.

'Will Moscow be covered in snow?' asked one child.

'If you find the little girl, give her our love!' called another.

'Goodbye, goodbye!' Mr Carmichael called back to his large family. 'Believe me,

I'd much rather stay at home with you!'

I wonder who the little girl is? thought Sara from the shadows as she watched Mr Carmichael setting off on the long journey to Moscow in search of the lost daughter of Captain Crewe.

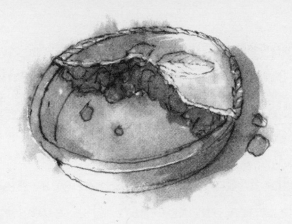

10

The Magic

As Sara turned to go into her house she paused for a moment to look into Mr Carrisford's sitting room. Cold and wet as she was, she could draw a little warmth from it before delivering her shopping to the cheerless kitchen. She was only just in time, because Ram Dass was closing the shutters against the darkness outside.

Sara couldn't have known that Ram Dass had had a busy afternoon and wanted to report on it to his master. And she would have been amazed to know that while Mr Carrisford was waiting for news from Mr Carmichael he had asked Ram Dass a lot more questions about the girl in the attic next door. Ram Dass watched over his little friend Sara more than she ever knew, and he was able to tell Mr Carrisford about this extraordinary child and the way she managed to survive by making the best of things and telling herself stories. Between them they had cooked up a plan. That very afternoon, Ram Dass had paid a visit to Sara's little room and taken notes on what he saw . . .

Wearily Sara handed her parcels to Cook. 'I'm surprised you didn't stay out all night,' said Cook crossly.

'May I have something to eat?' asked Sara. A single bun is not enough to keep a growing child going all day.

'Certainly not,' said Cook. 'Tea's over and done with.'

'I had no dinner,' said Sara, feeling weak with hunger.

'Then fetch yourself some bread from the pantry,' said Cook, knowing that only hard crusts remained.

Sara barely had the strength to climb all the stairs to her room that afternoon, but she was pleased to see a light under her door, which meant that she had a visitor.

'Ermengarde!' she said. 'Let me change out of my wet clothes and wrap myself in my bedcover. Then I can tell you more stories about the French Revolution.'

The two girls were sitting on Sara's bed when they heard a voice that made them freeze. 'Miss Minchin!' whispered Ermengarde, wide-eyed.

'Ssh!' whispered Sara back. 'She's telling Becky off for something. She won't bother to come in here.'

They heard a slap and Miss Minchin shouting, 'Half a meat pie, indeed! You deserve to go to prison for stealing!'

Then Miss Minchin's footsteps could be heard going downstairs, and Becky crying in the next room: 'It wasn't me! It's always Cook. I don't steal! I'm that hungry – but I don't steal!'

Sara was white with rage. How she hated injustice! 'Becky doesn't steal,' she said to Ermengarde. 'Cook steals food, but Becky doesn't, even though she's so hungry she'll eat crusts from the rubbish sometimes.'

Ermengarde watched her friend and a thought came to her. 'Sara,' she asked timidly, 'I've never liked to ask before, but are you ever – hungry?'

She was taken aback when Sara replied, '*Yes!* I'm so hungry now I could almost eat you! But Becky's even hungrier than I am.'

Ermengarde was thinking. 'Oh, Sara,' she

said, 'how stupid of me! I have a whole hamper of food in my room that my aunt sent me today. Why don't I go and fetch it? You can have as much as you like!'

'All right,' said Sara, feeling faint at the thought of food, 'but don't get caught!'

'I won't,' said Ermengarde and she crept downstairs, leaving her red shawl behind in her haste.

Sara knocked on the wall and soon Becky was at her door, still red-eyed and tearful. Sara spread Ermengarde's shawl on the table. 'There,' she said, 'we're going to have a banquet. Come on, Becky, let us set the table!' Soon Becky was caught up in Sara's story. 'I will call upon my Magic,' said Sara dramatically. 'I know, my Magic has told me to look in the trunk.'

Sara's old trunk was empty but for a few useless bits and pieces. 'These hankies can be our gold platters!' said Sara, laying them round, 'and these –' she pulled some artificial flowers off a battered old hat, 'are our garlands.'

She used the flowers to decorate her tooth mug and her soap dish. Soon Becky was imagining the beautiful banqueting hall, complete with minstrels in the gallery and a huge fire burning in the grate.

Ermengarde returned with her hamper. 'Doesn't it all look lovely!' she said, and the girls started to put the food on the table.

'One more thing!' said Sara. 'Let's have a real fire for a few minutes – just to make it perfect.' And when she'd lit a few bits of rubbish in the grate, they each helped themselves to a piece of delicious cake.

But then they stopped with the food halfway to their lips. Miss Minchin's footsteps were heard on the stairs for the second time that evening. She threw open the door.

'So, Lavinia was right, Ermengarde.' She caught sight of Becky and boxed her ears

yet again. 'As for you! Go to your room. I'll deal with you in the morning.' Becky crept out, shoulders shaking.

'We – we were only having a party,' said Ermengarde hopelessly.

'So I see,' said Miss Minchin. 'I wonder what your father will say when he hears where you are tonight?'

Then she turned to Sara. 'This could only have been your idea, Sara. You shall have no breakfast, dinner nor supper tomorrow as a punishment.'

She saw that Sara had that strange expression again. 'Sara? What are you thinking of?'

'I was wondering,' said Sara.

'And what were you wondering, you dreadful child?'

'I was wondering,' said Sara, 'what *my* father would say if he heard where I was tonight.'

Miss Minchin grabbed Sara by the

shoulders and shook her furiously. 'How dare you! How dare you!' she shouted. Then she swept all the food back into the hamper and hustled Ermengarde out with it. 'I shall leave you to wonder!' she said to Sara and shut the door.

Sara hugged Emily. 'There is no banquet, Emily,' she said. 'I can't pretend any more. Perhaps I can sleep and pretend in a dream.' She sat and stared at the empty grate. If she'd looked up at that moment she might have seen a kind face at the skylight, but she carried on talking to her doll: 'Imagine a lovely fire there, with a comfortable chair by it – and a little table all laid with a hot supper.'

She climbed between her icy sheets and pulled the thin cover over her. 'And imagine that this is soft and warm and comfortable . . .' Sara fell asleep.

* * *

About an hour later something woke Sara. She wasn't to know that it was the skylight clicking shut. She lay there, not quite awake. She was warm and comfortable. Warm and comfortable? She must still be dreaming.

I don't want to wake up, she thought. This is such a nice dream.

Then she heard the gentle crackling of a fire in the grate. She opened her eyes and looked around. 'I can't be awake!' she said.

She was looking at a blazing fire with a little brass kettle hissing. There was a soft warm rug in front of the fire and a folding chair with cushions on it. By the chair was a folding table covered in a white cloth, a teacup and a teapot and several covered dishes. There were warm fleecy covers on her bed and a quilted silk dressing-gown hanging above matching slippers – all lit by the light from a lamp with a rose-coloured shade.

Sara couldn't believe her eyes. 'It can't be true!' she cried, 'but it all seems so real!' She put on the dressing-gown. 'It's warm and soft. It feels real.' Then she went over and held out her hands to the fire. 'A dream fire wouldn't be hot,' she said.

She came upon a pile of books and carefully opened the top one. Someone had written: *'To the little girl in the attic. From a friend.'* Suddenly Sara burst into tears. 'Somebody cares about me,' she sobbed. 'I have a kind friend.'

Sara went into Becky's room. 'Wake up Becky, come and see!' Becky sat up, startled at the sight of Sara as she used to be, in a fine silk dressing-gown. Sara took Becky into her room. 'It's real, Becky! The Magic came and did it!'

What a wonderful evening the two hungry girls had. They sat by the fire and ate sandwiches and soup and toast and muffins. They didn't know who had done this, but Sara knew that someone was looking after her. And then they went back to bed, Becky taking some of Sara's new blankets, and slept as well-fed, warm children do.

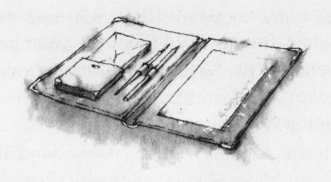

11

The visitor

By the next morning the whole school seemed to know that Sara and Becky were in serious trouble and that Sara was to be starved for the day. They watched her closely for signs of suffering. Miss Minchin hoped that maybe Sara's proud spirit would be broken at last.

But Sara had a spring in her step, and a smile hovered around her lips. It puzzled Miss Minchin.

Sara saw Becky in the kitchen and they laughed together when no one was watching. 'We have to keep our Magic a secret, Becky,' said Sara. 'It would be too awful if Miss Minchin found out.'

That night Sara was up late working and then studying. She felt a little afraid as she stood outside her attic door. What if it had all been a dream? What if everything had disappeared again?

But there it all was! Sara looked around in wonder. The Magic had been again! A fire burned in the grate and supper was laid on the table for her – and for Becky as well this time. A box had been turned into a sofa with a rug and cushions. The walls had been decorated with pretty bits of material and there were ornaments on the shelves. The two girls ate their food in front of the fire and when they went to bed Sara found that she had a new soft mattress. I'm living in a fairy story, she thought as she fell asleep.

* * *

And every day after that, though Miss
Minchin was cruel and Cook sent her out
into the cold on endless errands, Sara could
survive by looking forward to what she
would find when she opened the door
of her attic bedroom. It might be a new
book, or a pretty tablecloth, a lamp or a soft
covering. When she was being sneered at
by Lavinia or punished for something
that wasn't her fault, Sara just thought to
herself, If only you knew . . . The fairy story
was even better than one she might have
invented herself.

After a few weeks of good food and
warm beds, both Becky and Sara started to
fill out and get stronger. Miss Minchin took
no notice of Becky, but when she saw Sara
looking better each day, it worried her.

'Most girls,' she said to her sister Amelia,
'would be humble by now. I don't like
Sara's defiance. It's not right in a servant.'

Then one day something very exciting happened. Sara answered the door and took in a parcel. 'Take it to the girl to whom it is addressed,' said Miss Minchin crossly as Sara lingered in the hall.

'It – it's addressed to me,' said Sara in a shocked voice.

'What do you mean? No one sends you

parcels! How can it be addressed to you?'

'It says, "TO THE LITTLE GIRL IN THE RIGHT-HAND ATTIC" – and that's me.'

'Well, open it up, then. There must be some mistake.'

But there was no mistake. Inside the parcel were some beautiful warm clothes in just Sara's size, a coat and warm shoes, even a hat and an umbrella. A note said 'TO BE WORN EVERY DAY. WILL BE REPLACED WHEN NECESSARY.'

Miss Minchin was a little frightened. What if some cross guardian were suddenly to turn up? What did all this mean? She looked nervously at Sara and tried to sound kind. 'You'd better put the clothes on, then. And when you're dressed, you can come back into the schoolroom for your lessons. There'll be no more errands today.'

Imagine the surprise for the other girls, when the scruffy servant appeared as

Princess Sara again! Perhaps Sara was going to turn out to be a princess after all.

Becky noticed that Sara was very quiet that night as they ate their supper by the fire.

'Are you inventing something, miss?' she asked. 'Are you going to tell me a story?'

'I'm thinking, Becky. I would so love to thank whoever is doing this for us. The Magic has been so kind. But how can I thank someone when I don't know who it is?' She looked around the little room that had been made so pretty. Then her eye fell on a beautiful writing case and pens that she'd found only two days earlier.

'Why didn't I think of it before!' she cried. 'I'll write a letter and leave it where they can find it.' Without further ado she sat down and wrote a note.

'I hope you don't mind me writing to you when I know you want to stay secret. I

*only want to thank you for being so kind
and making everything like a fairy story
for Becky and me. We used to be so cold
and hungry and lonely – and look at us
now! Please let me say, 'Thank you –
thank you – thank you!'*
THE LITTLE GIRL IN THE ATTIC.'

She left the letter on the table the next
morning and when she came back in the
evening it had disappeared. She and Becky
sat by the fire again, Sara reading from one
of her new books. As they sat there they
heard a strange scrabbling sound. It wasn't
Melchisedec because it came from the
skylight.

'It's the monkey!' said Sara. 'Oh, poor
thing, it's far too cold for it out there!'

She stood on her table and opened the
skylight carefully so as not to frighten the
monkey. She spoke softly to it and coaxed
it in. The little creature cuddled up to her

and clung on to her hair.

'There, there, little thing,' she said. 'I'll let you sleep on my bed tonight, but tomorrow I'll have to take you back next door where you belong.'

12

The little lost girl

The next day Sara raced through her chores as quickly as she could, so that she could return the monkey to the Indian gentleman. Little did she know that it was a very important day for Mr Carrisford, because today Mr Carmichael would return from Moscow with the little lost girl.

In fact, Mr Carrisford was in such an agitated state that the older Carmichael girls and little Donald were there to keep him company.

'We already like the little lost girl so much,' said Janet. 'We can't wait to meet her.'

'Did you tell Mr Carrisford about the little-girl-who-isn't-a-beggar?' interrupted Donald. 'How someone has bought her some nice new clothes? Perhaps she's been found, too.'

Just then a cab drew up outside and the three children rushed to the door crying, 'Papa! It's Papa!' Mr Carrisford followed them anxiously with his eyes. 'But there's no little girl!' said Donald.

Mr Carmichael made his way into the room. 'Children, go and play with Ram Dass for a few minutes while I talk to Mr Carrisford alone.'

'So you didn't find her?' asked Mr Carrisford. He looked crestfallen and ill again.

'I eventually tracked down a child

called Emily Carew in Moscow,' said Mr Carmichael. 'I met her, but she is younger than the girl we are looking for. I'm sorry.'

'Then we must start the search again at once,' said Mr Carrisford. 'But where?'

'Well, I was thinking that perhaps we should start here, in London,' said Mr Carmichael.

'There are plenty of schools in London,' said Mr Carrisford. 'Why, there's one next door!'

'Let's start there then,' said Mr Carmichael.

'There is a child next door who interests me,' said Mr Carrisford. 'But she is a little, dark, sad thing – not at all like Crewe.'

Perhaps the Magic was at work again, for at that very moment Ram Dass was coming into the room. 'The child herself is here,' he said. 'She has returned the monkey. I asked her to stay, because I thought you might like to speak to her.'

'Who is this child?' asked Mr Carmichael.

'Heaven knows,' said Mr Carrisford, and went on to explain how he and Ram Dass had helped the little girl in the attic.

Sara came in. The monkey clung to her affectionately. She spoke to Carrisford in her pretty voice. 'I would have brought him back last night,' she said, 'but I knew you weren't terribly well, so I didn't want to disturb you.'

'That was very thoughtful of you,' said Mr Carrisford, looking at her with interest. 'He seems to like you.'

'Oh, I'm used to monkeys,' said Sara. 'I was born in India, you see.'

Mr Carrisford sat bolt upright. Sara felt quite startled.

'You live at the school next door?' he asked. 'But you are not a pupil?'

'I don't know quite what I am,' said Sara. 'I was a pupil, but now I sleep in the attic and run errands for the cook.'

Mr Carrisford looked feverish. 'Question her, Carmichael,' he said.

Mr Carmichael smiled kindly at Sara. 'Tell me, my dear,' he said, 'what happened?'

'When my papa died, he lost all his money, so no one could take care of me – except Miss Minchin.'

'And she made you into a servant?'

'There was no money – and nobody.'

'How did your father lose his money?' asked Mr Carrisford breathlessly.

'It was his friend,' said Sara. 'His friend took his money and ran away.'

'Tell me,' said Mr Carrisford. 'What was your father's name?'

'Ralph Crewe,' said Sara. 'He died in India.'

'Carmichael!' shouted Mr Carrisford. 'It is the child – the child we've been looking for these last two years!'

'What child am I?' asked Sara.

'Mr Carrisford was your father's friend,' said Mr Carmichael.

* * *

Mr Carrisford needed to rest, so Janet took Sara into another room and her mother came to join them.

'He isn't really a bad man,' explained Mrs Carmichael. 'The worry made him ill, you see – he wasn't in his right mind when he ran away. And he had no idea you were the lost child – he just wanted to make you happier.'

Sara looked puzzled. Mrs Carmichael went on, 'so he told Ram Dass to bring the things to your attic. He is kind and good.'

'So he told Ram Dass –?' said Sara, as Mr Carmichael called them back in again.

Now Sara ran straight to Mr Carrisford and stood by his chair. 'It was you!' she said. 'You, who sent me the beautiful things! You are my kind friend!' And she knelt down and kissed the thin hand.

'Look – the man is changed already,' said Mr Carmichael to his wife, as they saw Mr Carrisford smile.

There were to be many changes. It was decided that Sara would never go back to Miss Minchin's. 'I will go and speak to her,' said Mr Carmichael, but he was saved the trouble because Miss Minchin rang at the door at that moment. Cook had reported seeing Sara going next door with something under her cloak.

She bustled in. 'I do apologise,' she said.

'I don't know what the girl was thinking of. Go home at once, Sara. You will be severely punished.'

'From now on her home will be with me,' said Mr Carrisford.

Miss Minchin looked about her wildly. 'With you? With you, sir? What can this mean?'

Mr Carmichael explained to Miss Minchin that Mr Carrisford was a friend of Mr Crewe and that half his fortune from the diamond mines now belonged to Sara.

'There are not many princesses,' he told her, 'who are richer than your "errand-girl". Mr Carrisford has found her at last, and he will keep her.'

'But Sara,' wheedled Miss Minchin, 'don't you want to come home? I've done everything for you. You would have starved, but for me.'

'You know why I won't go home with you, Miss Minchin,' said Sara steadily.

Miss Minchin grew angry. 'You won't see your friends ever again—' she started.

'I don't expect any parents will forbid their daughters to visit an heiress,' said Mr Carmichael, and Miss Minchin knew she was beaten.

'Huh!' she sneered at Sara, 'I expect you feel you're a princess again now.'

'I tried not to be anything else,' said Sara, 'even when I was at my coldest and hungriest.'

Miss Minchin flounced home and complained to Amelia. 'It's all your fault,' said Amelia, bold for once. 'We'll be ruined once it gets out how we treated Sara.'

That evening Ermengarde held up a letter in the schoolroom. 'It's from Sara,' she said. 'She was a princess after all.' And somehow Miss Minchin knew that no one would be obeying any rules that night.

Becky heard it all. It's over, she thought. No more firelight. No more stories. Tears blurred her eyes as she crept up to her room. She stood outside, knowing that all the Magic would have disappeared with Sara. But when she opened the door, Ram Dass was waiting for her.

'Sara hasn't forgotten you,' he said. 'First thing tomorrow you are to come and live next door with her,' and he slipped away, back through the skylight.

Sara and Mr Carrisford – or Uncle Tom, as he asked her to call him – became the best of friends. Soon she heard his side of the Magic, and the Carmichael children loved to hear the whole story over and over again. Still he gave her gifts, including a large dog called Boris, who arrived with a note round his neck saying '*I come to serve the Princess Sara.*'

One evening Sara was unusually quiet.

'What are you "supposing", Sara dear?' asked Mr Carrisford.

'I have an idea,' said Sara. 'I want to go back to the bakery where the lady was so kind to me, and set up a fund so that she can give buns to starving children.'

So the next day they set off for the bakery.

'Of course I remember you,' said the woman in the bakery. 'And I want you to meet someone. Anne?' she called.

And there was the beggar girl, well fed now, working in the back room. 'I took her in that very day. She's a good girl, and now she works for me and lives here.'

Sara told them both about her plans to feed hungry children.

'I should like it,' said Sara to Anne, 'if you'd be the one to give away the buns, because you know what it is like to be hungry.'

'Yes, miss,' said Anne, and Sara drove away knowing that she and the beggar-girl understood one another very well.

Alice in Wonderland

By Lewis Carroll
Adapted by Susan Holliday

One day Alice follows a white rabbit down a rabbit-hole, and finds herself in a strange new world where animals can talk. She shrinks smaller than a mouse and grows taller than a tree, runs in a Caucus Race, and goes to a Mad Hatter's tea-party. But will she be able to escape the Queen of Hearts . . . ?